My Little Friend®

GOES TO THE DENTIST

By Evelyn M. Finnegan

Illustrations by Diane R. Houghton

LITTLE FRIEND PRESS

SCITUATE, MASSACHUSETTS

First U.S. edition 1995.
Printed in China. Published
in the United States
by Little Friend Press,
Scituate, Massachusetts.

ISBN 0-9641285-1-9

Library of Congress
Catalog Card Number: 95-077741

Second Printing

LITTLE FRIEND PRESS
28 NEW DRIFTWAY
SCITUATE, MASSACHUSETTS 02066

*To my daughter Lynne whose kindness and
love have touched the hearts of many.*

*To my granddaughter Katherine whose
life has filled our hearts.*

Just before I go to
bed I brush my teeth.

"Katherine, how is
that front tooth?"
asked Dad.

"It feels so wiggly
I can't wait for it
to come out."

"Mom, why won't this wiggly tooth come out like my others?"

"Well," said Mom, "some teeth just need a little extra help to come out, Katherine. That's why you and Nana are going to see the dentist tomorrow."

The next day, I put on my
favorite sweater, the one Nana
made especially for me.
Inside it has a secret pocket with
a seatbelt for My Little Friend.

It's such a beautiful day we decide
to walk to the dentist's office.

"How nice to see you again Katherine," said the dental assistant.

"I'll tell the dentist you're here."

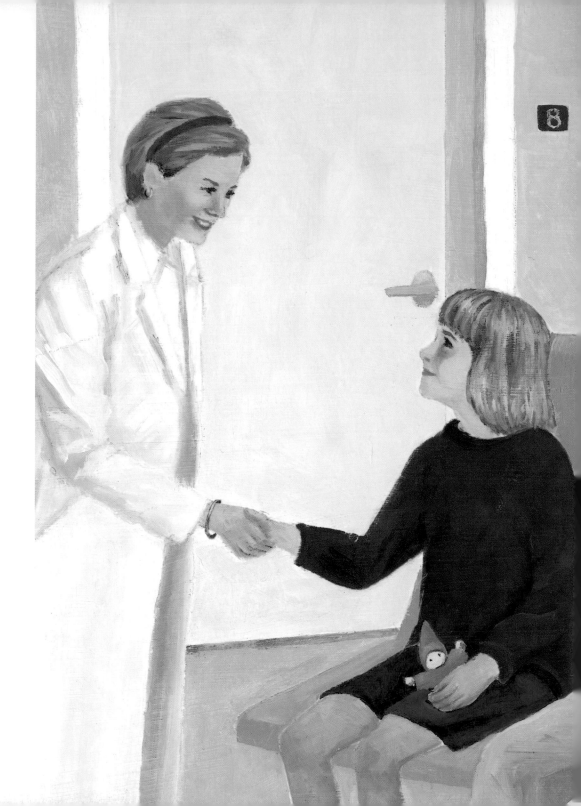

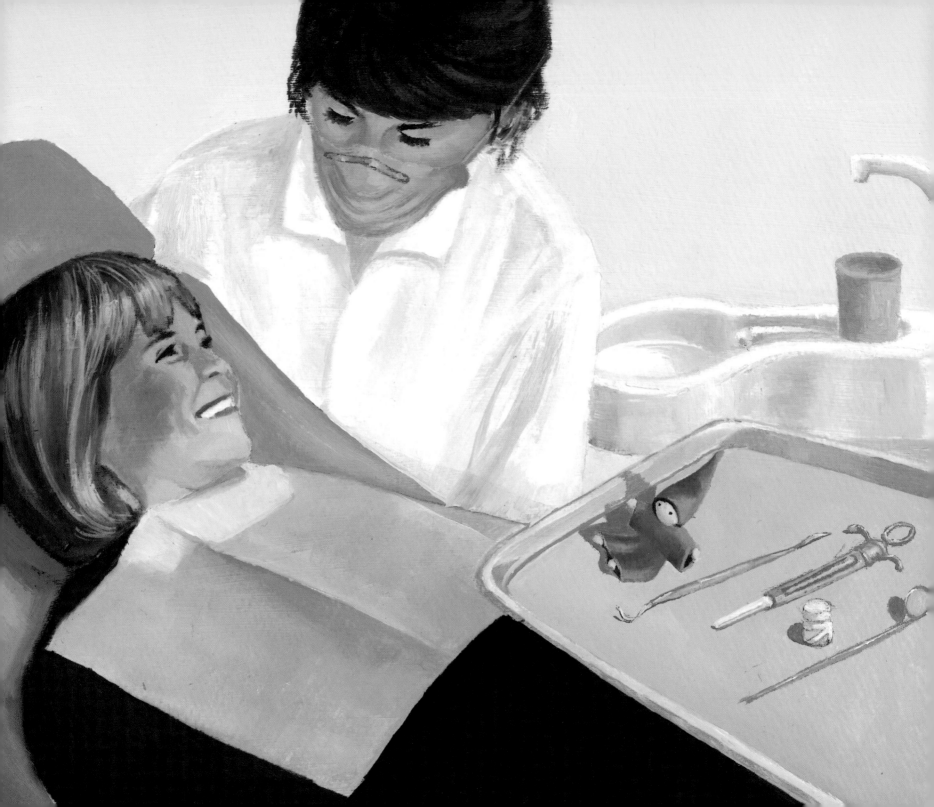

"Hello Katherine."

"Hi Doctor Hills."

"I'm glad to see you again," said the dentist.
"Why don't we put your Little Friend up on
the bracket table to watch us?"

"That's a good idea," I said.

"Open *real* wide," said Doctor Hills,
as she used the curved mirror to
look at all of my teeth.

"How many teeth do I have?"

The dentist used her explorer to count
each one and said, "twelve on the top
and twelve on the bottom."

"Twenty-four," I said.

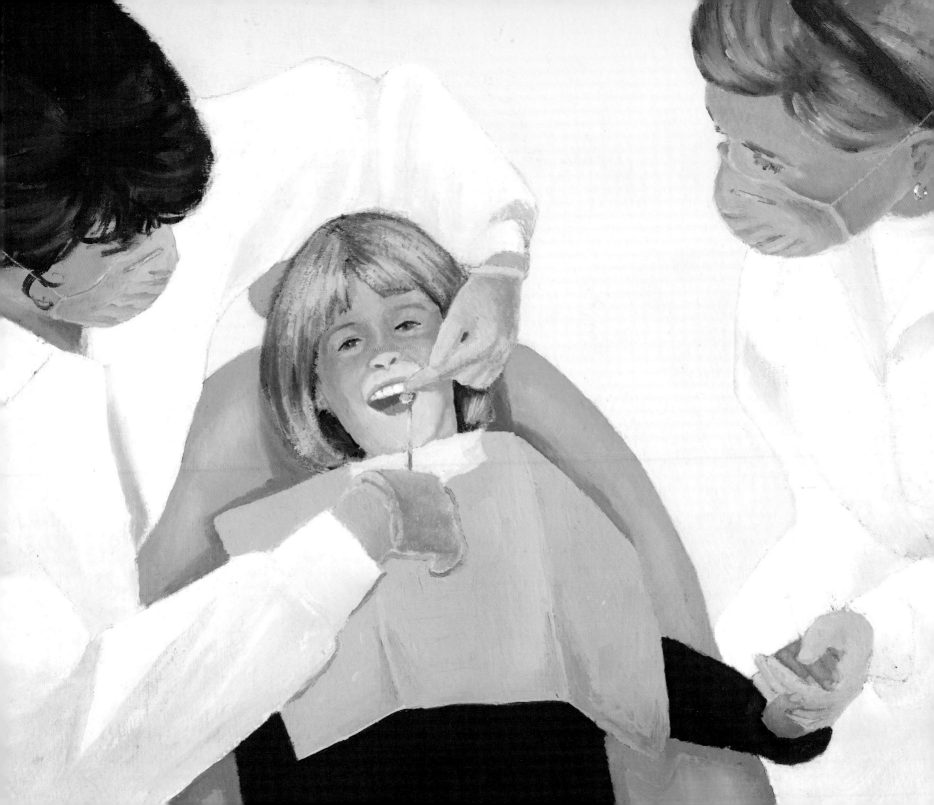

"It looks like your wiggly tooth could use some extra help to make a space for your new tooth Katherine."

"How? Will it hurt?"

"You'll hardly feel it," said Doctor Hills. "First I use this long cotton swab with yellow gel to help put your gum to sleep."

"Mmm, it tastes like a banana," I said.

"Next you'll feel a pinch as I give you an injection of sleepy juice. Once it starts to feel numb I can take out your tooth."

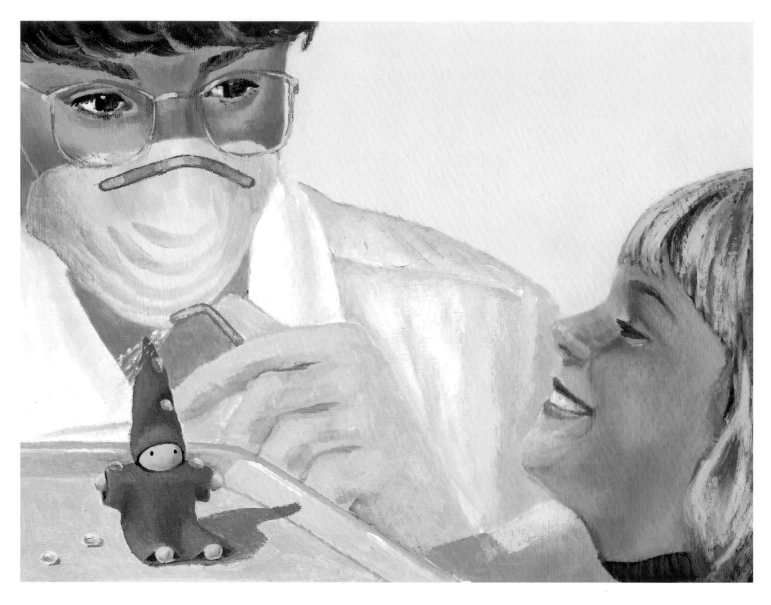

The water spray tickles and makes a
swish sound as she rinses out my mouth.

"The gauze helps me to clean off your wiggly tooth," said Doctor Hills.

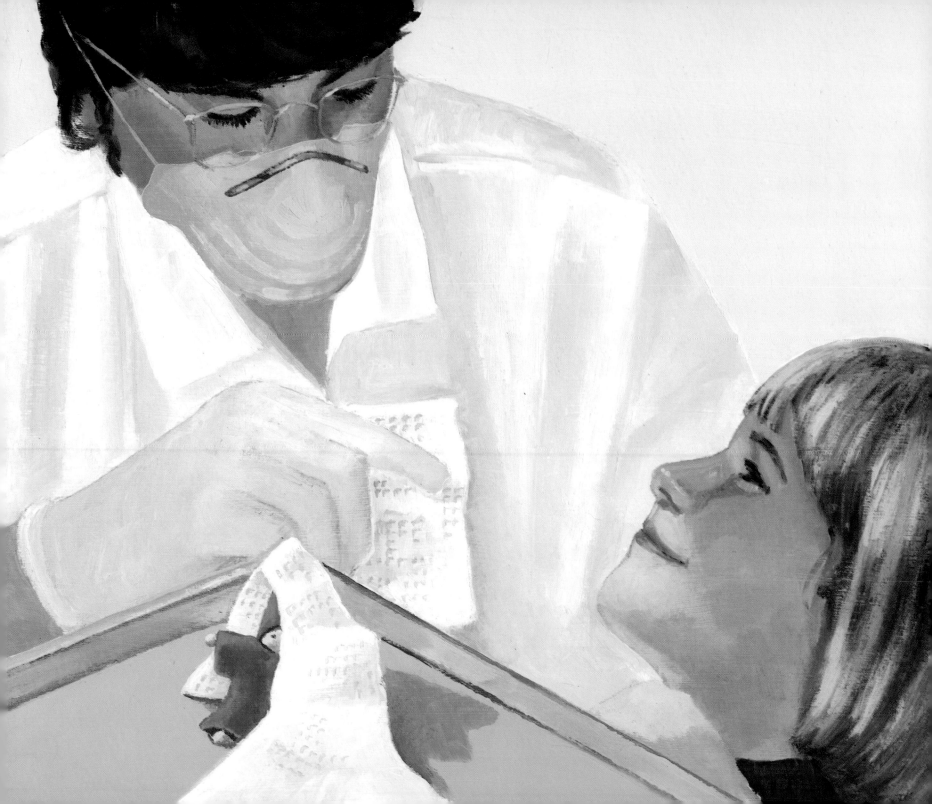

"Now I'll use the air syringe to dry off your tooth. It's wet in there you know."

And the air syringe made a loud sound like the *howling* wind.

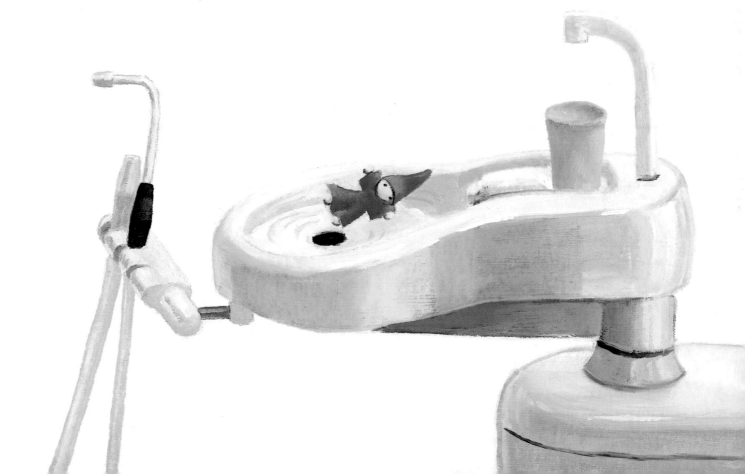

"Then I felt a little pull in my mouth."

"All done...here it is!" said Doctor Hills.

"Be sure to put it under your pillow tonight."

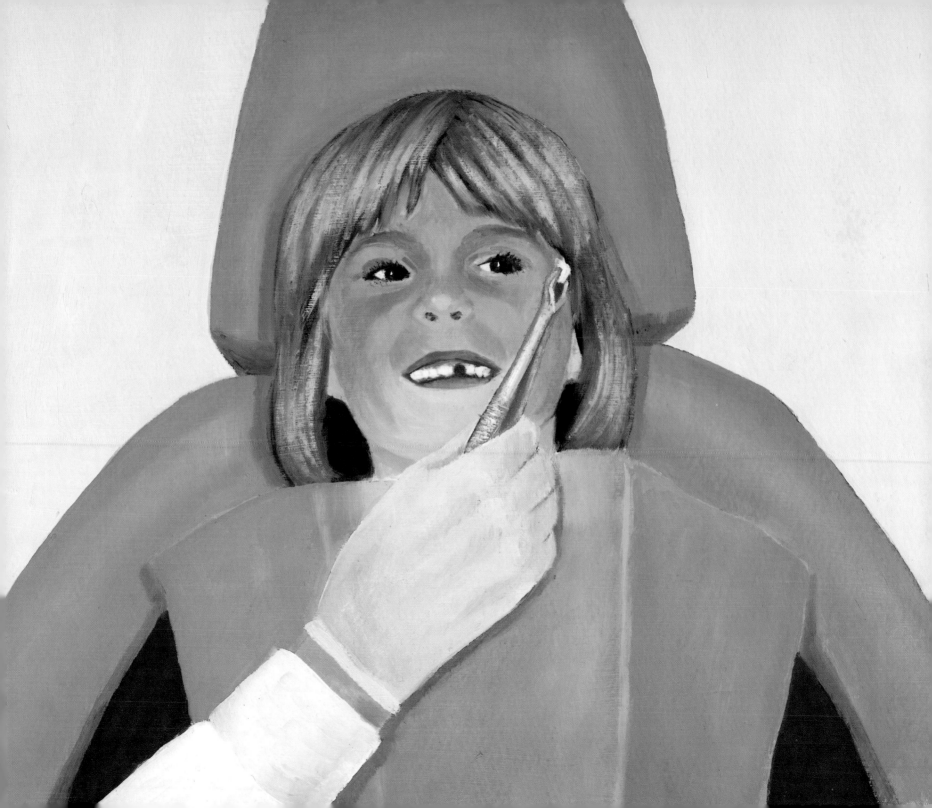

I was happy showing my tooth to the other children.

As we started to leave I remembered My Little Friend was still on the bracket table.

"I have to go back and get My Little Friend."

I looked, but My Little Friend wasn't there!

I looked under the chair.

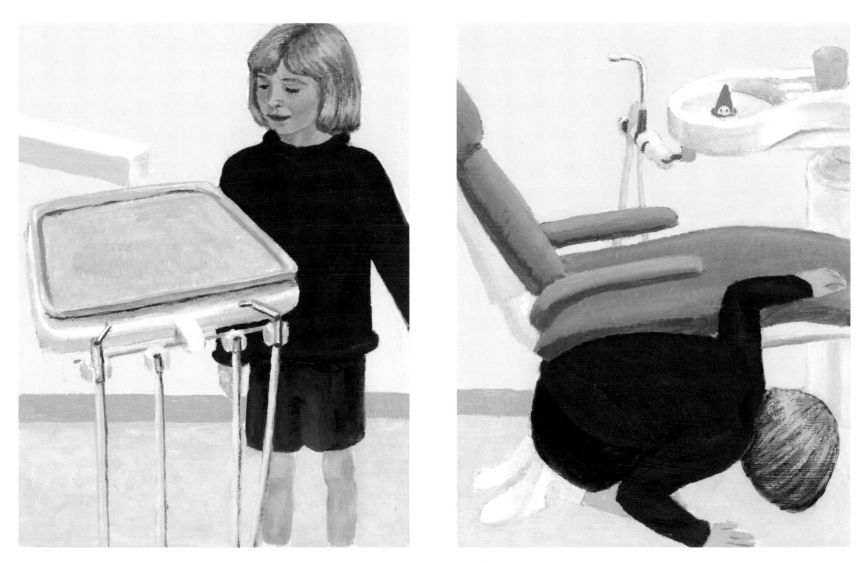

I looked in the trash.   And I looked on the floor.

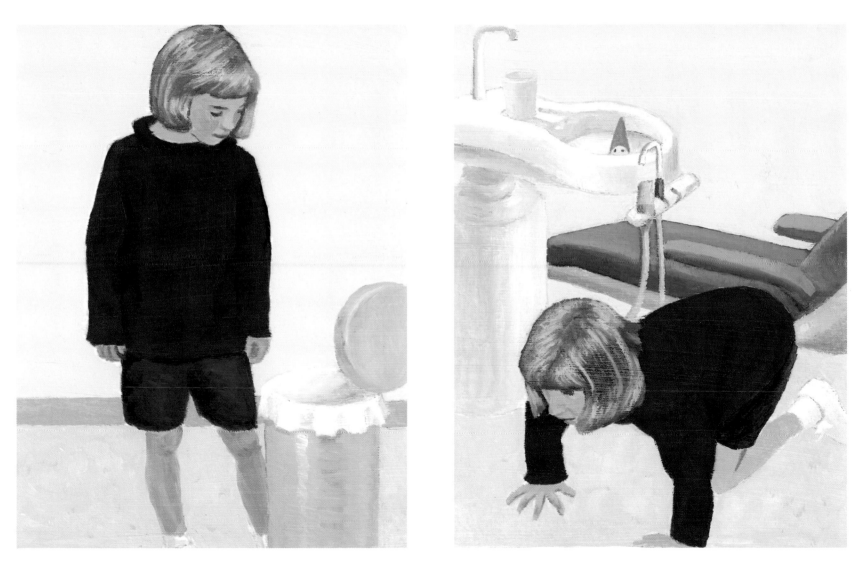

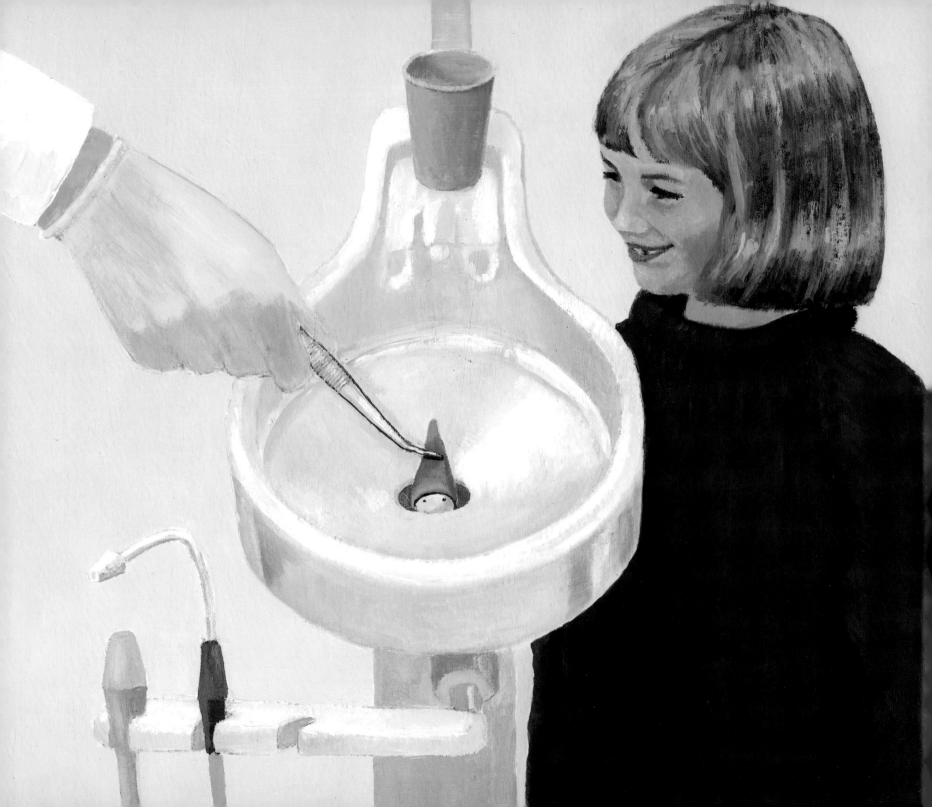

Suddenly, Doctor Hills said,
"Well look who is in the cuspidor!"

And using her pliers, she carefully
lifted out My Little Friend.

"Oh Little Friend what a silly place
for you to be. I better dry you off."

That night I put My Little Friend and
my tooth together in a special place.

Can you guess where?

GLOSSARY

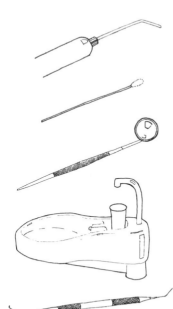

Air syringe — *a small tube like tool that blows air*

Cotton swab — *a small piece of cotton on a stick used to apply gel to your gums*

Curved mirror — *a long handled mirror to help the dentist see all around the inside of your mouth*

Cuspidor — *it looks like a small sink — you can rinse out your mouth with water then spit in it*

Explorer — *a pointed tool that acts like the dentists' fingers to check for any cracks or cavities in your teeth*

Gauze — *a very thin cotton, loosely woven material*

Pliers — *just like tweezers for picking up small objects*

Sleepy juice — *liquid medicine that is injected into your gum or cheek so you won't feel pain*

Water spray — *a fine mist of water*

Yellow gel — *it is applied to your cheek or gums so you won't feel the injection—it looks and feels like jelly and comes in many flavors*